Dear Parents:

Congratulations! Your child is taking the first steps on an exciting journey. The destination? Independent reading!

STEP INTO READING® will help your child get there. The program offers five steps to reading success. Each step includes fun stories and colorful art or photographs. In addition to original fiction and books with favorite characters, there are Step into Reading Non-Fiction Readers, Phonics Readers and Boxed Sets, Sticker Readers, and Comic Readers—a complete literacy program with something to interest every child.

Learning to Read, Step by Step!

Ready to Read   **Preschool–Kindergarten**
• big type and easy words • rhyme and rhythm • picture clues
For children who know the alphabet and are eager to begin reading.

Reading with Help   **Preschool–Grade 1**
• basic vocabulary • short sentences • simple stories
For children who recognize familiar words and sound out new words with help.

Reading on Your Own   **Grades 1–3**
• engaging characters • easy-to-follow plots • popular topics
For children who are ready to read on their own.

Reading Paragraphs   **Grades 2–3**
• challenging vocabulary • short paragraphs • exciting stories
For newly independent readers who read simple sentences with confidence.

Ready for Chapters   **Grades 2–4**
• chapters • longer paragraphs • full-color art
For children who want to take the plunge into chapter books but still like colorful pictures.

STEP INTO READING® is designed to give every child a successful reading experience. The grade levels are only guides; children will progress through the steps at their own speed, developing confidence in their reading. The F&P Text Level on the back cover serves as another tool to help you choose the right book for your child.

Remember, a lifetime love of reading starts with a single step!

Educators and librarians, for a variety of teaching tools, visit us at RHTeachersLibrarians.com

Library of Congress Cataloging-in-Publication Data is available upon request.
ISBN 978-0-593-18126-3 (pbk.) — ISBN 978-0-593-18127-0 (trade) —
ISBN 978-0-593-18129-4 (lib. bdg.) — ISBN 978-0-593-18128-7 (ebook)

Printed in the United States of America
10 9 8 7 6 5 4 3 2 1

This book has been officially leveled by using the F&P Text Level Gradient™ Leveling System.

PJJ
BLUE

Rocket Finds an Egg

Pictures based on the art by Tad Hills

Random House 🏠 New York

It is a sunny day!

Rocket and Bella play
in the meadow.

Rocket stops.

He finds an egg!

Rocket and Bella
search the meadow.

They see Owl.

"Is this your egg?"

Rocket asks.

"No," Owl says.
"My eggs are
all here."

Rocket and Bella
find a bluebird.

The egg is not hers.
Her eggs are blue.

They ask
the little yellow bird.

The egg is too big
to be hers.

The friends ask
a bird with spots.

Her eggs
have spots.

They ask a red bird.

They ask a black bird.

They ask a brown bird.

They can not find
the egg's home!

Rocket and Bella
ask the chickens,
"Is this your egg?"

"No, it is not our egg,"
the chickens say.

At the pond,
the friends ask
the ducks.

The egg is not theirs.

"I am tired,"

Bella tells Rocket.

They take a break.

Then they hear

a SPLASH!

"My egg!"
a turtle says.
"That is my egg!"

"It is a turtle egg,"
Bella says.

"I looked for it
all day,"
the turtle tells them.

"We are glad
you found us!"
Rocket says.

Rocket and Bella
follow the turtle
to her nest.

At last,

the egg is home.